Ready For Reading!

LEVEL 1

Dear Parents,

Congratulations! Your child has embarked on an exciting journey – they're learning to read! As a parent, you can be there to support and cheer them along as they take their first steps.

At school, children are taught how to decode words and arrange these building blocks of language into sentences and wonderful stories.

At home, parents play a vital part in reinforcing these new-found skills. You can help your child practise their reading by providing well-written, engaging stories, which you can enjoy together.

This series offers exactly that, and more. These stories support inexperienced readers by:

- gradually introducing new vocabulary
- using repetition to consolidate learning
- gradually increasing sentence length and word count
- providing texts that boost a young reader's confidence.

As each book is completed, engaging activities encourage young readers to look back at the story, w̲ reinforces new vocabulary. Enjoym together can be great fun for both

Prue Goodwin
Lecturer in Literacy and Children's Books

D1350858

How to use this series

This series has 4 levels. The facing page shows what you can expect to find in the books at each level.

As your child's confidence grows, they can progress to books from the higher levels. These will keep them engaged and encourage new reading skills.

The levels are only meant as guides; together, you and your child can pick the book that will be just right.

Here are some handy tips for helping children who are ready for reading!

Give them choice – Letting children pick a book (from the level that's right for them) makes them feel involved.

Talk about it – Discussing the story and the pictures helps children engage with the book.

Read it again – Repetition of favourite stories reinforces learning.

Cheer them on! – Praise and encouragement builds a child's confidence and the belief in their growing ability.

LEVEL 1 For first readers

* short, straightforward sentences
* basic, fun vocabulary
* simple, easy-to-follow stories of up to 100 words
* large print and easy-to-read design

LEVEL 2 For developing readers

* longer sentences
* simple vocabulary, introducing new words
* longer stories of up to 200 words
* bold design, to capture readers' interest

LEVEL 3 For more confident readers

* longer sentences with varied structure
* wider vocabulary
* high-interest stories of up to 300 words
* smaller print for experienced readers

LEVEL 4 For able readers

* longer sentences with complex structure
* rich, exciting vocabulary
* complex stories of up to 400 words
* emphasis on text more than illustrations

Make Reading Fun!

Once you have read the story, you will find some amazing activities at the back of the book! There are Excellent Exercises for you to complete, plus a super Picture Dictionary.

But first it is time for the story . . .

Ready?

Steady?

Let's read!

Tim Warnes

Can't You Sleep, Dotty?

LITTLE TIGER
LONDON

Dotty could not sleep.

So she started to howl.

"Try counting the stars,"
said Pip.

But Dotty could only
count to one.

AWoooooooo

"Have a little drink,"
said Susie.

So Dotty had
a little drink.

Slurp!
Slurp!

But then she made a puddle.

AWOOOOOOOOOO...

"I hide in my burrow at bedtime," said Whiskers.

Wag!
Wag!

So Dotty dived under
her blanket.

But it was too dark.

"I like to sleep where it is sunny," said Tommy.

Plod
Plod

Dotty liked that idea . . .

. . . so she turned on her torch!

Poor Dotty. Then Tommy
had an idea. All Dotty
needed was . . .

. . . a cuddle!
Night night, Dotty.

Excellent Exercises

Have you read the story? Well done!
Now it is time for more fun!

Here are some questions about the story. Ask an adult to listen to your answers, and help if you get stuck.

Sleepy Dog

Dotty cannot get to sleep! What do *you* do to help you fall asleep?

Top Toys

Can you name Dotty's toys in this picture? What toys do *you* like to take to bed?

Pip's Plan

Now describe what Dotty is doing in this picture.

Night Night!

Can you remember how Dotty falls asleep at the end of the story?

Picture Dictionary

Can you read all of these words from the story?

blanket

cuddle

howl

night

puddle

sleep

stars

torch

under

whiskers

Can you think of any other words that describe these pictures – for example, what colours can you see? Why not try to spell some of these words? Ask an adult to help!

Fred

Fred has a new little door. It's called a cat flap. But Fred knows that Horrible Henry is waiting outside, ready to pounce . . . !

My Turn!

When Oscar and Tilly go to the playground, they are not keen to wait their turn. Will the two friends find a way to play together?

Rosie's Special Surprise

Nosy Rosie likes to know everything about everything. So when Daddy Rabbit says he has a special surprise, she hops off to look for it. Whatever could it be?

What Bear Likes Best!

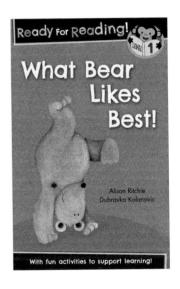

Bear really likes to have fun. But all of his friends are busy and he keeps getting in the way! Will it ever be time to play?

For Noah x

LITTLE TIGER PRESS LTD,
an imprint of the Little Tiger Group
1 The Coda Centre, 189 Munster Road, London SW6 6AW
First published in Great Britain 2001
This edition published 2017
Text and Illustrations copyright © Tim Warnes 2001, 2013
Visit Tim Warnes at www.ChapmanandWarnes.com
All rights reserved
Printed in China
978-1-84869-730-0
LTP/1800/1856/0417
2 4 6 8 10 9 7 5 3 1

More books from Little Tiger Press!

LEVEL 1 – For first readers

Can't You Sleep, Dotty?

Fred

My Turn!

Rosie's Special Surprise

What Bear Likes Best!

LEVEL 2 – For developing readers

Hopping Mad!

Newton

Ouch!

Where There's a Bear, There's Trouble!

The Wish Cat

LEVEL 3 – For more confident readers

Lazy Ozzie

Little Mouse and the Big Red Apple

Nobody Laughs at a Lion!

Ridiculous!

Who's Been Eating My Porridge?

LEVEL 4 – For able readers

The Biggest Baddest Wolf

Meggie Moon

Mouse, Mole and the Falling Star

The Nutty Nut Chase

Robot Dog